Blizzard

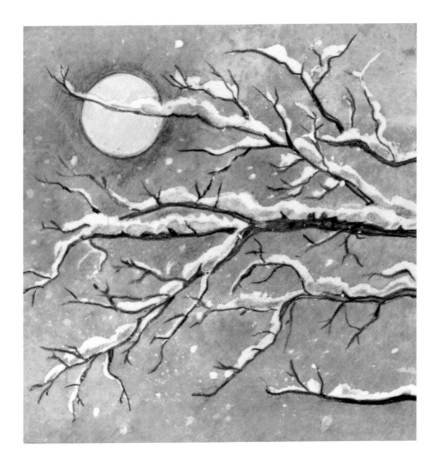

Carole Gerber
Illustrated by Marty Husted

𝒹 Whispering Coyote
A Charlesbridge Imprint

A **Whispering Coyote** Book
Published by Charlesbridge Publishing
85 Main Street
Watertown, MA 02472
(617) 926-0329
www.charlesbridge.com

Library of Congress Cataloging-in-Publication Data
Gerber, Carole.
Blizzard/Carole Gerber; illustrated by Marty Husted.
p.   cm.
"A Whispering Coyote Book"
Summary: A raging winter storm contrasts with the cozy atmosphere of a
young boy's home.
ISBN: 1-58089-064-4 (reinforced for library use)
[1. Snow—Fiction. 2. Bedtime—Fiction. 3. Stories in rhyme.]
I. Husted, Marty, 1957-ill. II. Title.
PZ8.3.G297 Bl 2001
[E]—dc21   00-043829

Printed in Hong Kong
(hc)10 9 8 7 6 5 4 3 2

Illustrations done in watercolors and color pencil on Arches cold press watercolor paper
Display type and text type set in Publicity Gothic Solid, Goudy Old Style,
and Goudy Old Style Italic
Separated and manufactured by Toppan Printing Co.
Book production by *The Kids at Our House*
Designed by *The Kids at Our House*

To Sara Paige DeLacey, with love from Mimi
—C. G.

To my father, Frank Hoffelt, with gratitude
—M. H.

Outside, the ground is cold and white.

Inside, my home is warm and bright.

Outside, a snowstorm swirls and blows.

Inside, the fireplace toasts my toes.

Outside, the snow is piling up.

Inside, hot cocoa fills my cup.

Outside, the snow surrounds a tree.

Inside, a soft quilt covers me.

Outside, white drifts are everywhere.

Inside, I snuggle in a chair.

Outside, the wind slows, then grows still.

Inside, I climb up on the sill.

Outside, I see it's gray and white.
A snowy blanket wraps the night.
Stars gleam bright in a vast, dark sky.
The moon's round face drifts slowly by.

Inside, I rinse my cocoa cup.
I take my quilt and fold it up.

Then I put on my winter boots . . .

my scarf . . . my mittens . . . my snowsuit.

Outside, I lean back toward the snow,
stretch out my arms—
and down I go!

I flap my arms, jump up, and then admire my silent snowy friend.

Inside, I change and wrap up tight.
Outside, my angel sleeps.

Goodnight!